For
Toni
who loves boots!
Anne Turner
1998

KATIE'S TRUNK
by Ann Turner
illustrations by Ron Himler

Macmillan Publishing Company
New York

Maxwell Macmillan Canada
Toronto

Maxwell Macmillan International
New York   Oxford   Singapore   Sydney

Macmillan Publishing Company is part of the Maxwell Communication
Group of Companies.

Macmillan Publishing Company
866 Third Avenue
New York, NY 10022

Maxwell Macmillan Canada, Inc.
1200 Eglinton Avenue East
Suite 200
Don Mills, Ontario M3C 3N1

Printed in China

10   9   8   7   6   5   4   3   2

The text of this book is set in 14 pt. Kennerly Old Style.
The illustrations are rendered in watercolor and pencil.

Library of Congress Cataloging-in-Publication Data
Turner, Ann Warren.
Katie's trunk / by Ann Turner ; illustrations by Ron Himler. — 1st ed.
p.   cm.
Summary: Katie, whose family is not sympathetic to the rebel soldiers during
the American Revolution, hides under the clothes in her mother's wedding
trunk when they invade her home.
ISBN 0-02-789512-2
1. United States—History—Revolution, 1775-1783—Juvenile fiction.
[1. United States—History—Revolution, 1775-1783—Fiction.]
I. Himler, Ronald, ill.   II. Title.
PZ7.T8535Kat   1992   [E]—dc20   91-20409

For my cousin Katie,
descendant of the original Katie
—A.T.

When I'd been bad all day long,
hiding Hattie's doll under the sofa
and never telling where it went,
Mama sighed and said, "I should sit you down
to sew long seams all day
and get the goodness straight inside,
Katie. What is wrong with you?"

I couldn't tell it with a name,
though I felt it inside,
the way a horse knows a storm is near.
I could feel the itchiness in the air,
the wind bringing cold,
the clouds tumbling over the trees
bringing rain—a sour rain.

"Must be," Mama sighed and sat down to tea,
"must be all this trouble and fighting.
Why, it makes me skittish as a newborn calf,
all this marching and talking,
these letters your Papa speaks of,
that tea they dumped in the harbor."

Mama's hand shook.

"Tea! In the harbor! Wasting God's good food."

Brother Walter said, "That's not the least of it.

It will get worse."

She peered at him.

"How could it be worse, Walter?"

Then she shut her lips on the words.

Already we had lost friends, neighbors,

families we had played with on the green

and helped with building their new barns.

Celia Warren no longer spoke to me.
Her brother, Ralph, no longer spoke to Walter.
Sometimes I heard that word hissed, "Tory!"
like a snake about to bite.
The rebels were arming, brother told me,
marching and drilling beyond the meadows.

I'll never forget the day they came.
The sun was hot on the mill pond
and Walter, Hattie, and I watched the dragonflies
peel their skins off on the long grass
and fly away.
Something like smoke rose over the road
and out of it Papa came running. "Get your mother!
Hide in the woods. The rebels are coming!"

We ran to the house,
Mama's face like a white handkerchief.
She shoved a piece of pork pie in our hands
and ran us out to the thick woods
where we could hide.
Crouched in the underbrush,
I felt like an animal in a trap. And suddenly
I was so mad I could not still myself.

I raced for the house,
Mama's fierce whisper trying to call me back.
I would not let John Warren and Reuben Otis
hurt our house and things. It was not right,
it was not just, it was not fair.

Inside our parlor, I touched each thing
I loved: Mama's pineapple teapot,
the silver tray, shining like a moon,
the pictures of all our kin
ranged across the wall—home.

Then I heard voices by the door,
Reuben Otis, John Warren, Harold Smith
and others, not our neighbors.
"This'll be fine pickings!"
They paused on the front step
and ripped the knocker off the wood.

I ran into Mama and Papa's room,
looking for a place to hide.
If they could steal, they could hurt as well.
There was Mama's wedding trunk,
big and black and domed.
I pulled up the trunk lid and hid under the dresses.
In the shut down darkness everything
was muffled and faraway. The door slamming.
Their footsteps next door in the parlor.

"English goods!" someone spat
and something hit the floor and broke.
My breath stuck in my throat.
Someone cursed. I heard Reuben say,
"Mr. Gray has money here. Look hard for it."

John Warren spoke of arms they would buy.
The air closed around my mouth
like a black cloth.

I bit my hand and prayed,
though I was never much good at that.
I thought my words might go up to God
like bubbles in a pond to the silver top
where they would burst. "Please, God,
don't let them find me, don't let them hurt us,
let me breathe."
The footsteps came closer, someone leaned against
the trunk. My breath got caught somewhere midst
my stomach and chest, and I could not
get it back. There wasn't enough air.
John Warren said, "Fine dresses and silver here."
He pulled up the lid and the sweet air rushed in.
I sucked in a breath as a dress was snatched out.
The rustlings drowned their words,
another dress went, and a hand touched me.
I wanted to bite it, to make him jump and shout,
but I stilled myself. Maybe he didn't know.
Suddenly, he shouted, "Out! The Tories
are coming. Back to the road! Hurry!"
He did not close the lid, and footsteps sounded
out the door.

Sudden quiet. My heart beat loud
as the horses galloping down the road.
Quiet as quiet, I crept
to the window and looked out. No one.
Puffs of smoke far down on the green.

A horse thudding past, riderless;
someone's hat blowing by in the gusty wind.
Would I ever play with Celia again?
Would I always wear this name, Tory, as if
it were written on my chest?

I sat down, hugged my knees
and began to cry.
Walter ran inside and hugged me so tight
my nose stuck to his shirt.
Mama, Papa, and Hattie came next,
white as the moon and as silent.
Only Mama scolded, "Katie! Leaving us
that way..." Her voice broke
and she sat beside me and stroked my hair.
Papa looked out the window. "It's not bad,
dear ones, just a skirmish.
No one's hurt that I can see."

Walter's mouth snapped open and then
shut tight. I wiped my eyes on his sleeve.
A sudden thread like a song
ran through my head. When Mama asked me
to sew straight seams to get the goodness straight
I knew I couldn't do it.
But John Warren had. When I hid
in the black stuffy trunk,
when my breath got lost in Mama's dresses,
he left the trunk lid up to let me breathe
and called the others away.

He'd left one seam of goodness there,
and we were all tied to it:
Papa, Mama, Walter, Hattie
and me.

DATE DUE
